The Keeper
and the Crows

AN
ORCA
YOUNG
READER

The
Keeper
and the
Crows

Andrea Spalding

ORCA BOOK PUBLISHERS

Canadian Cataloguing in Publication Data
Spalding, Andrea.
The keeper and the crows

ISBN 1-55143-141-6

I. Title.
PS8587.P213K43 2000   jC813'.54   C00-910194-2   PZ7.S737Ke 2000

Library of Congress Catalog Card Number: 00-100930

Orca Book Publishers gratefully acknowledges the support of
our publishing programs provided by the following agencies:
the Department of Canadian Heritage, The Canada Council
for the Arts, and the British Columbia Arts Council.

Cover design and interior illustrations by Kirsti

IN CANADA	**IN THE UNITED STATES**
Orca Book Publishers	Orca Book Publishers
PO Box 5626, Station B	PO Box 468
Victoria, BC Canada	Custer, WA USA
V8R 6S4	98240-0468

02 01 00 • 5 4 3 2 1

*For Jesse, who can keep secrets,
and for Carrie and Terry
and their inspirational Gingerbread Cottage.*

As always, many people have played a role in this book.

Thanks to Bob, Christine, Susan and the rest of the wonderful staff at Orca; Ann Featherstone, the best editor I've ever worked with; my husband Dave, without whom the book literally wouldn't have been written; and Morgan Bartlett, the honest kid who read and commented on the first draft.

A special thank you to Pat and Reg Kerford, whose Lake Ontario cottage allowed me time and space to finish the first rough draft.

Chapter One

"CAW, caw ... Alert, alert!" The watching crow set up a piercing call that startled all the other crows in the area. Answering in a great cacophony of sound, the others rose from their roosts in the nearby trees and wheeled around in a black spiral against the blue sky. Two hundred beady eyes fixed on the little red car far below, and the small figure of a woman hurrying across the gravel drive toward it.

"Be ready, ready," called Watcher anxiously. His brother Swiftwings swooped out of the spiral and glided high above the

car, poised to follow wherever the car went.

With a puff of smoke from its exhaust and a cloud of dust from the gravel, the little car backed smartly out of the cottage drive and headed off down the road, Swiftwings in attendance.

"Caw, caw ... it's open, open," Watcher called as he flew to the cottage window ledge. He tapped smartly on the glass with his beak to indicate the entry point, fluttered back to the fence, and took up his watch again.

Shaggy but mystically white, the albino crow called Old One flew slowly forward and perched arthritically on the ledge. Though stiff and ragged, there was no doubt he was a force to be reckoned with. His red eyes shone with a bright intelligence. The other birds grew silent as they watched.

Head cocked to one side, Old One listened. No sound came from the cottage. He stepped forward, one foot at a time, until he was within the gap of the open window.

There was a gasping caw of disbelief

from one of the young crows wheeling above as Old One stepped inside the human's cottage and disappeared from view.

Silently the spiral above wheeled around and around, watching and patiently waiting.

The GO train rolled to a stop at the end of the line. Misha grabbed his bag and tumbled down the steps, feeling relieved and important. He'd done it. Traveled on his own from Toronto to meet up with his favorite aunt.

His eyes glanced anxiously along the length of the small country platform, but there were too many commuters between him and the ticket office for him to catch a glimpse of her. He wove rapidly back and forth through the crowd toward the station entrance. There she was. Relieved, he ran the last stretch, dropped his bag with a big thud, and gave her a bear hug.

"Wow, Misha," said Aunt Dora. "You've

grown. I hardly recognized you." She ruffled his hair.

Embarrassed, Misha brushed his hand over his hair and quickly rearranged it.

Aunt Dora chuckled. "Sorry, I'll try to remember not to do that again." She eyed his bulging sports bag. "Do you need a hand?"

"Nope." With a happy grin Misha hoisted the bag, followed his aunt to the car park, and waited while she unlocked the trunk.

"It was cool … Dad made sure I got on the right train — then all I had to do was sit there." He laughed. "I didn't even have to remember which stop to get off at because this is the end of the line." Misha slung his bag in the trunk and slammed it shut. He looked curiously around at the rolling Ontario farmland beyond the station. "So … how far to your new cottage?"

Aunt Dora smiled. "About fifteen minutes — but it's not new … it's almost 130 years old."

"Neat. Does it have any secret passages or anything?"

Aunt Dora shook her head. "None that I've found," she said, opening the car door for him then going around to the driver's side. "Not unless you count the root cellar. It's hidden by a door set in the kitchen floor."

"Brilliant," said Misha with satisfaction. "I'll help you explore it — hey, look at that." He laughingly pointed to a large crow perched on the fence by the car, head on one side and eyes fixed on them. "That crow looks as though he's listening to us."

Misha sat down and firmly slammed the door. The crow soared up from the fence and disappeared. Misha was so busy fastening his safety belt that he missed the look of concern that crossed his aunt's face.

Inside the cottage, Old One was searching. It was harder than he'd anticipated.

"The Box, the Box?" he croaked under his breath. It wasn't going to be easy, for there were unusual boxes everywhere. Dora was a collector of boxes, and they covered almost every available surface. There were music boxes and jewelry boxes, papier mâché boxes from Kashmir, and glass boxes from the Czech Republic. Boxes of silver and boxes of gold jostled in groups on wooden box trunks acting as coffee tables. Découpage boxes marched across window ledges, and shell-covered boxes huddled on dressers. Old One looked carefully at them all, nudging some with his beak. He gave a rumble of dissatisfaction deep in his throat. None of these boxes had a lock that looked right. He'd never seen it; he'd only heard the stories handed down from previous Old Ones. But his story was different — he had the key as proof.

"Caw, caw, alert, alert." Watcher's call echoed through the house.

Startled, Old One flapped his white wings and fluttered quickly through the rooms *back to the kitchen. Old One alighted on the kitchen counter, hopped onto the drain rack and perched precariously on the pots and pans. He stepped over the battered wooden recipe box and up onto the window ledge. Edging carefully through the crack of the open window, he spread his wings and soared over the garden to the fields beyond.*

"He's back, back," cawed Watcher happily. The spiral above disintegrated into black fragments as the relieved birds returned to their roosts in the maples.

The little red car swung into the driveway, and Dora and Misha climbed out.

"Welcome to the village of Belfountain and my Gingerbread Cottage," said Dora with a smile as they both entered the house.

Chapter Two

"This cottage is really neat." Misha ran from room to room checking everything out. His footsteps echoed on the polished pine floorboards. "The floor isn't flat, there are waves in it," he called.

Dora laughed. "The boards have warped with time and I think the foundation has sunk a little. It makes walking fun."

Suddenly Misha's footsteps were still. "Hey, Aunt Dora," he called. "Have you got a pet cockatiel?"

"No," called back Dora. "Why?"

Misha reappeared in the kitchen holding

a white feather. "I found this on the dining room floor."

Dora took the feather and twirled it between her fingers. "That's odd. It wasn't there earlier, and none of the dining room windows are open."

"Maybe it blew in through the kitchen window and the draft swept it in there," suggested Misha helpfully.

"Maybe," said Dora. She walked over to the kitchen window and examined the sill. There was nothing to see. But as she turned back to Misha, she gave a start and bent down to examine a mark on one of the shiny pans upended in the drain rack.

"What are you looking at?" Misha walked over to the counter.

Swiftly Dora's arm shot out and rubbed over the bottom of the pan, but not before Misha caught sight of a bird's footprint. He watched, puzzled, as Dora looked at the open window again, then opened it further and leaned outside.

In the tree opposite, Misha saw a crow staring.

The bird and Dora seemed to stare at each other for a long time, until, with a flutter of leaves and wings, the crow left his perch and soared away with a disdainful *CAAWW*.

Dora shook her head as if to clear it and turned to Misha.

"What's with that crow?" he asked.

"Nothing. It's just a little cheeky. You're right, the feather must have blown in — have you discovered the back stairs yet?" she asked abruptly.

Misha looked startled. "Back stairs? I've found the front ones … you mean there are others?"

Dora pointed to a tall cupboard door in the wall. Misha opened it. "Wow, you *do* have a tiny secret passage!"

"Not really. This is the old servants' staircase to the small back bedroom. It was built out of the way in a kitchen cupboard."

"Okay. So where's the secret cellar?" Misha looked down at the kitchen floor. "I can't see anything."

"You'll have to help me." Dora grabbed one end of the kitchen table and gestured Misha to hold the other. Together they lifted it to one side. Aunt Dora knelt down and rolled up the rag rug. There was the outline of a door cut in the floor, complete with a brass ring sunk into its boards.

"Can I?" Misha looked questioningly at his aunt. She nodded again.

Misha bent down, lifted the ring and pulled. Softly and sweetly the door rose to one side. A black hole yawned at his feet. A set of narrow wooden steps descended into the darkness.

"There's a light switch to the right of the top step," Dora said.

Misha bent again, and his hand fumbled by the step and clicked a switch.

The root cellar sprang into view — a perfectly ordinary, small whitewashed cellar. Shelves lined each wall and a chest freezer stood at the far side. Baskets hung from a couple of ceiling hooks, and jars of jams and pickles jostled for shelf room with tins of tomatoes and other household staples. Everything sparkled with cleanliness and order.

Misha sighed with disappointment. "It really isn't a secret room, it's just kitchen storage."

His aunt nodded. "'Fraid so."

"But it looks like it should be a secret room. Maybe there is a hidden passage." Misha launched himself down the stairs and enthusiastically began knocking on the walls between the shelves to see if they sounded hollow.

"Careful. Don't knock things over," cautioned Dora.

Misha hammered again in one area. "Listen ... it sounds different here." He stood back and critically surveyed the wall, then knocked again. "That piece of wall looks different from the others. I bet it's a boarded-up secret passage."

Dora shook her head. "Sorry, but this really *is* just an old root cellar. Previous owners took part of the wall down to run wires behind. That was when electricity was brought in some years ago."

Misha's face fell. He knew in his heart Dora was right, but he'd always wanted to find a secret tunnel, and they were non-existent in Toronto.

"Guess it would look different without the light," he said.

"Want to try?"

Misha nodded.

Dora flicked the switch and lowered the door. Misha was plunged into darkness.

The darkness was heavy and complete. It pressed around him like a heavy cloak threatening to smother him.

His heart thumped. His skin suddenly felt clammy.

"Aunt Dora," he croaked. "Please open the door."

Immediately the door was lifted back, and a comforting shaft of daylight spilled into the cellar. Misha leaped back up the steps and pressed the light switch.

"You okay, Misha?"

Misha nodded but stared back down into the brightly lit cellar. "Guess I didn't know how black darkness is. I've never been in complete darkness before. There are always street lights in Toronto."

"Sorry, I didn't mean to scare you," said Dora, her expression full of concern.

"It's okay … it was just black." Misha grinned up at his aunt. "We could keep a treasure box down here, though, couldn't we?" he added. "We could pretend it *is* a secret dungeon because there's only you and me who know about it. Who would think of moving the table and rolling up the rug to find the cellar?"

Dora laughed. "In these old houses, I think lots of people have a door in the floor. But you're right. Kids your age wouldn't know. We'll both choose something special to keep down there." Dora walked over to the window ledge and picked up a long, narrow enameled box with a hand-painted soldier on the lid. She opened it and placed the white feather inside. "There." She passed the box to Misha. "Now you place a treasure inside and hide it in the root cellar."

Misha took the box and ran his finger admiringly over the soldier. "Awesome … how old is it?"

"That was made in the seventeenth century — it's about two hundred years old."

"Wow … you have some really old boxes in your collection, don't you, Aunt Dora?"

A strange look flitted across Dora's face. "Yes, I certainly do," she said briskly. "Now hurry and find something to add to that one; then we can get my kitchen to rights again."

High on the cottage roof, perched on the top of the old chimney, Swiftwings was

listening intently. The old wood-burning kitchen stove was long gone, but the stovepipe was still in place. It ended in a grille in the kitchen ceiling, and the two voices from inside the house floated effortlessly upward.

"Caw, caw ... She knows, she knows," called Swiftwings. "Found Old One's feather, feather ... There's a secret room, room. Call Council! Call Council!"

"Council ... Council ..." The other crows took up the cry until the woodland across the field echoed with their voices. They rose from their roosts and blackened the sky with a soot-like smudge as they streamed toward the oldest maple tree.

The Old One held court. "The key is OURS," he insisted.

"Ours ... ours." The crows nodded in agreement.

Old One dropped his voice and his whisper became more sinister. "We must not fail."

"Fail ... fail ..."

"The ancient power should always have been given to the crows. Now is our chance to find it."

"Find it … find it." The crows clacked and clattered their beaks in agreement, and the branches of the maple shook as though in a gust of wind.

"But the child … the child?" asked Watcher fearfully.

The Old One glared around with his red eyes and stretched out his still powerful wings in a threatening posture. "He must not get in the way. Scare him …"

"Scare him … scare him … scare him … scare him …" The crows gleefully took up the cry and rose, circling above the giant maple in a tornado of wings as they scattered back to their roosts.

★★★

"Boy, those crows sure are noisy," said Misha, coming back into the kitchen.

His aunt was staring out of the window.

19

"Yes," she replied absently, "they are." She turned. "Ready to hide your treasure?"

Misha held out his hand. "My favorite fossil. It's an ammonite and it's millions of years old. I think it brings me luck, so it deserves to be kept safe in a secret place."

His aunt held the soldier box open, and Misha carefully placed the ammonite beside the feather and shut the lid. Then he clambered down the stairs and looked around.

The cellar was so tidy, there weren't any obvious hiding places, other than behind the rows of tins and jars. Doesn't really look like a secret dungeon with the light on, Misha thought, with a tinge of disappointment. It's not mysterious and there are no cobwebs or spiders anywhere. He peered over some large cardboard cases in the corner.

"Aaah, that's more like it."

The cases concealed a part of the paneled wall that was coming away from the corner stud. Misha spotted a gap behind just big enough for his box.

He opened the lid, took out his lucky ammonite and turned it over and over in his palms. He whispered softly so Dora wouldn't overhear. "I wish I could find a real secret passage somewhere and have a proper adventure, like kids in books."

Misha swiftly replaced the ammonite in the painted box and closed the lid, then knelt down and tucked the box inside the gap.

Now it's really hidden, he thought, as he pushed the cardboard cases back against the gap, then clattered happily up the stairs. "Okay, Aunt Dora, our treasure box is safe."

Together Misha and Dora unrolled the rug and dragged the table back in place. Misha smiled with satisfaction. "See, now no one will ever guess there is a secret dungeon."

His aunt grinned, reached out her hand

to Misha's head, then snatched it back quickly.

Misha laughed up at her. She'd remembered. "Now, tell me more about the gingerbread cottage, and why this village is called Belfountain."

Chapter Three

"The gingerbread is easy to explain," said Aunt Dora as they walked out into the late-afternoon sunshine to the front of the old cottage.

"Look up at the eaves, just around the roof, and all around the top of the porch, Misha. What do you see?"

"You mean all that lacy wood stuff?"

"Exactly. That's known as gingerbread trim. I decided to call this the Gingerbread Cottage because there is so much of it and because it makes the cottage look like a fairy-tale cottage."

"Like the witch's cottage in *Hansel and Gretel*, but without the candies," agreed Misha.

"But Belfountain … now that's a different story."

Misha looked up eagerly. His aunt always had an odd story or two.

"There's a park down the hill containing the ruins of an old mansion. In its grounds is a lawn and a lovely moss-covered fountain."

"Neat," said Misha with satisfaction, "Bet that's where the name comes from. It sounds kind of French. My teacher said *belle* means beautiful. Is the village called Beautiful Fountain?"

"No, I don't think so. The village was called Belfountain before the mansion was built." Dora hesitated. "I wondered if it was a French name for the springs that come up in the valley. *Belle fontaine* — beautiful springs. It's really pretty where the river runs through the grounds of the mansion." Dora laughed. "You'll love it. There are the remains of secret passages and grottoes built into the banks."

Misha's eyes sparkled.

"But there is also a story that involves an actual bell," continued Dora. "It is said that in a time of danger, a bell will ring to warn the villagers. When the bell rings, the river is supposed to rise and encircle the village to keep it safe. Unfortunately, no one knows where the bell is, or how it makes the river rise."

"Great," said Misha with satisfaction. "I love exploring. I'll look for the bell, so it can ring and save you if trouble breaks out."

Dora laughed. "That will certainly keep you busy." She looked around at the lengthening shadows. "It's getting late. You'll have to explore tomorrow."

"Okay. Can I watch TV?" Misha asked.

His aunt shook her head and spread her hands.

Misha looked at her in disbelief. "You're joking, right? You're not going to stop me from watching TV."

"I don't have one. Sorry."

Horrified, Misha gazed at his aunt. "But ... but ... what do you do in the evenings?"

"Read, do jigsaw puzzles, talk to friends, work on some crafts. Lots of things."

"But ... but ... what about *The Adventures of Hercules,* or *The Simpsons*? And ... and ... the hockey playoffs?"

Dora shrugged and laughed. "They get on fine without me." She placed her arm around Misha's shoulder. "It's not such a big deal, is it ... you've got books with you?"

Misha nodded. "I guess so ... I've just never been anywhere without a TV."

"It will be good for you then," said his aunt, giving him a gentle squeeze. "You'll just have to rely on your imagination." She pointed to a large bush covered in foamy white blossoms. "There's an elder tree. If your imagination isn't working, try picking a few blossoms and dropping them into the water when you wash your face. Herbalists say it helps you see interesting things."

"Sometimes you're weird, Aunt Dora," said Misha, returning her hug. "But I get the point. I'll go and unpack my books."

Misha walked over to the elder tree, sniffed at the blossom and wrinkled his forehead. He looked across to his aunt. "You don't believe that stuff, do you?"

Dora smiled and bent down to pull a stray weed.

Misha pulled at the spray, and the branch bent before suddenly parting with the blossom and snapping back. The tree shook, and a crow burst from its hiding place. Cawing wildly, it angrily dive-bombed Misha.

Startled, Misha wrapped his arms over his head and ran for the porch.

Still cawing, the crow veered away.

Shocked and puzzled, Misha watched it go. "It attacked me," he blurted out. "Why? I don't hurt birds."

Dora shook her head. "I guess you frightened it," she said slowly.

"And why do I feel like it was watching us?" asked Misha, still upset.

Dora sighed. "Probably because it was. Crows have many human traits — one of them is curiosity. As I'm new here, they're probably checking me out."

Misha snorted in disbelief. "No way — they're birdbrains."

Dora shook her head. "Crows are highly intelligent. They also love bright objects and will find and steal shiny things, then keep them in a secret hoard."

Misha looked over the wall and across the field toward the far woods where the crow had taken refuge. "Lots of your boxes are shiny, Aunt Dora," he said thoughtfully. "Do you think they are after one of those?"

"Crows would have trouble picking up a box," she replied with a stilted laugh, but she shaded her eyes and joined Misha to look across the field.

Misha realized he was still holding the elder spray. It was wilting rapidly. He wandered back into the kitchen and stuck it in a jar full of water, then looked around for somewhere to place it.

The kitchen was crowded. Pots and pans, beautiful bowls full of fruit, garlic braids, and bunches of herbs all jostled for space with Dora's boxes and other jars of flowers. Misha shrugged, opened the cupboard door and carried the jar up the hidden, twisted back stairs to his bedroom. He placed the jar on the window ledge.

It was a small room with a slanted ceiling tucked under the house eaves, but Misha liked it. It had more angles and character than his box-shaped bedroom at home. Misha sat on his bed and unpacked the books from his pack. He'd brought four — all action adventure stories — but today they seemed to have lost their appeal. Somehow this little room — in fact, the whole house — seemed to ooze hidden stories of its own, different from those in his books. Maybe more exciting.

Suddenly the room seemed stuffy and oppressive. Misha walked over to the small window and fumbled with the net curtain to find the latch and open it further. He looked down ... and froze.

His room overlooked the backyard, a secretive place sheltered from passing eyes by large trees and bushes. In the far corner, a small stream trickled musically into a good-sized pond.

There was Dora, talking urgently to the pond.

Misha gazed in astonishment and gently pushed the window further open. He leaned forward to see and hear better.

"... if you could send word ... find out about the crows."

The water in the pond swirled, and a large white fish arched out of the water.

"Certainly, Keeper of the Box."

Misha gasped, dropped the curtain and stepped back into the shadows of the bedroom.

He sidled up to the window again and

peeped out through the edge of the curtain. The pond was still, and Dora was walking thoughtfully back toward the house, absently deadheading flowers as she passed.

Misha let the curtain drop gently back and sat on the edge of the bed. "Spying crows, a warning bell, and an aunt who talks to fish," he mused. "Kind of an interesting holiday. Now, how do I get involved?" His eyes wandered thoughtfully around the room and landed on the spray of elder flowers.

He picked it up, shut his eyes and scrubbed it across his face. "Okay, let's see if the old folk stories are true." He grinned and dropped the crushed blossoms back in the jar.

Chapter Four

Supper took forever. Misha waited for Dora to say something, but she talked about everything but the pond. Maybe he'd imagined it. Misha wasn't going to say anything — he felt uncomfortable about eavesdropping.

"Would you like to feed my fish?" she finally asked as they washed up together after supper.

Misha's eyes shone. About time! Now she'd introduce him to the talking fish.

They walked through the garden and across stepping stones over the stream.

At the far side of the pond, they stood on a large flat rock jutting out over the water.

Dora gestured. "The pond's pretty shallow in most places, except for the middle, where it looks darker."

Misha peered. The light was going and it wasn't easy to see a change in the color of the water.

"That's 'the Deep.'"

"The Deep?" echoed Misha. There was something in Dora's voice that made the name sound secret and special.

"It's a crack through the inner rocks of the earth. It's so deep, no one has been able to measure it. Fresh water wells up through it, and sometimes a bubble or two of gas."

As they watched, a large ovoid bubble wobbled up from the depths and burst on the surface with a soft gaseous pop.

Dora reached into her pocket and brought out a small plastic bag containing pellets. She handed it to Misha. "If you stamp on the rock three times, the fish will come. Then scatter these on the surface."

Misha looked at her, then firmly stamped three times with his boot.

There was a stirring in the depths. Suddenly the pond was full of fish. Slinky brown trout swam in fluid figures of eight beneath the rock. He tossed the pellets and they scattered like rain on the water. With a flurry, at least twenty fish heads broke the surface, greedily gulping. Then the pellets were gone. Misha's shoulders sagged with disappointment. None of the fish was very big, and not one of them was white.

"I was hoping the Giant White Fish would come," he said sadly.

Dora gazed at him intently. "I thought I saw the curtain flutter," she murmured. Then she knelt down, cupped her hand over her mouth and called softly over the water:

"Alive without breath
As cold as death

Never thirsty, always drinking
Clad in mail but never clinking
Ancient One, hear my cry
Help us so that Hope won't die."

Misha stared intently at the water for what seemed like ages. Nothing happened.

Misha looked around. Dora had disappeared. He just glimpsed a flicker of her skirt around the bushes toward the house. Uneasily Misha looked down into the water again. It was twilight now, and the pond lay heavy and black at his feet. Misha shivered with apprehension. He opened his mouth to call out.

A stirring in the depths swirled upward. Misha's mouth snapped shut.

A gigantic white fish appeared, swimming in slow, pale circles beneath Misha's feet. Misha crouched down to see better.

The fish gazed up at him. Misha shivered; this fish was scary. Pale whitish pink eyes, enlarged by the water between them, swiveled upward to goggle into

Misha's eyes. Then the fish swirled. A row of fierce, sharp spines springing from its back ominously broke the surface of the water. Misha edged away.

The fish swam slowly past again. It seemed to fill the entire pond. As it passed the rock, it wafted the water surface with a long, ragged tail fin. Dark drops rained down on Misha. He wiped his face with his sleeve and wondered uneasily if he should take to his heels and run.

The fish circled several times, then finally came to rest at the edge of the rock, fins gently keeping it balanced, and tail waving to keep it stationary. Its pink eyes seemed to bulge, magnified by the water. Misha shuddered in revulsion. It was disgusting! He stared back down. The long grayish white body was covered in heavy scales like plates of armor. They were scarred and dented as though the fish was a survivor of many battles and skirmishes. The tail hung in tatters, and the snout was also scarred and puckered on one side. Then

Misha noticed a gleam in the fading light.

"Ouch," he gasped. "You've a great big fish hook caught in your lip." His hand reached out toward the sturgeon's head. "Would you let me remove it for you? I'll try and be gentle. Or I can get Aunt Dora to help."

"Thank you for your kindness," said the sturgeon, "but it's been there so long I almost forget about it. I'm the Ancient One. How can I help?"

Misha tried to collect his thoughts. "I'm ... I'm not sure," he stammered. "It was Aunt Dora ... she called ... see ... I saw her talking to you ... it's as though there's a secret with the crows ... I'd like to help if I can."

The Ancient One blew a couple of bubbles and circled the pond again. "You'll have to trust me."

"Okay," said Misha.

"Then jump into the water *now*."

Spellbound, Misha jumped.

Chapter Five

The shock of the cold water was over-whelming. Then other shocks followed in rapid succession. Misha's body grew smaller, became elongated and stream-lined. His legs transformed into back fins, his arms shrank to become front fins. Gills opened in his neck. Misha realized he was a living, breathing, swimming ... fish.

A tremor of fear shook his body.

"It's all right, Little One." The sturgeon's voice rumbled around the pond. "Don't be frightened. Just think like a fish, and follow me." A ragged fin ran comfortingly across Misha's back.

Misha felt the water around him surge as the gigantic white sturgeon's body began to slide past him and head toward the Deep.

"Help ... don't leave me." Misha gave a galvanizing twitch. To his surprise, his tail obediently swished rapidly from side to side, propelling him forward. His fins automatically compensated to keep him level as he swam to the center of the pond, lowered his nose, and altered the angle of his front fins. Down he plunged, following the Ancient One into the deep, dark crevasses of the earth.

Amazingly, it felt wonderful to have the water streaming and bubbling past him. Misha's fear receded. He'd always liked swimming but had never felt as exhilarated as this. Misha could feel currents of water moving beneath him. He could ride and bounce over them. Pond weeds floated past, gently caressing him. His scaly skin could sense how far he was

from the rocky walls of the crevasse.

The two fish descended rapidly, cutting through the deep watery recesses of the earth. It grew totally dark, but Misha realized that his fish senses didn't mind. Somehow he could "see" in the dark, but it was more like sensing than seeing. This world of swirling water tasted full of information as it flowed in through his mouth and out through the gills on the side of his neck. He instinctively knew how to avoid the strong currents and when his body could slip easily through a small gap. He could feel where the water was swirling against a rocky bump and fish-tail around it, and he could "taste" the scent of the great sturgeon he was following.

They swam deeper and deeper into the earth, then turned and eventually leveled off. The current moved sideways now, much slower. Side by side the Ancient One and Misha slid along a great river of darkness. Time and space were different in this world. Misha was still aware of up and down, but time and distance merged together. The flow of the current and the beat of his tail were what mattered here.

Misha suddenly sensed that the surface of the water was not far above. The two fish slowed and finally came to rest on a gravel bed. Misha's fish senses absorbed a picture of a giant underground body of water. It lay darkly silent in the bowl of an enormous limestone cavern soaring above. The place was as full of mystery as an ancient cathedral.

"Look above the surface," rumbled the Ancient One.

Misha floated upward off the gravel until he felt air on his scales and the surface of the dark water lapping along his sides. He swiveled his eyes upward.

The darkness was pierced by a single shaft of moonlight that fell in a straight line from the roof of the cavern to a small island in the middle of the underground lake. Its brilliance hurt Misha's eyes, and he turned away to rejoin the Ancient One.

"You saw the shaft of light and the island?"

Misha waggled his agreement.

The Ancient One sighed. "Who would have thought such a beautiful shaft of light could have brought us such trouble?" He settled sadly back into the gravel bed and indicated Misha should settle beside him.

"The world is threatened with an old danger," the Ancient One sighed again. "We need your help, but let me explain."

His great eyes swiveled toward Misha. "I apologize for bringing you here so suddenly. You adapted very well — it was a test of your courage, but I also had to be sure we could talk in a place of safety. A place no one would overhear and carry the information to the crows."

Misha wiggled excitedly. "So it *is* something to do with the crows ... I knew it! They've been watching Dora and the cottage ever since I arrived."

"Yes, it's the crows." The great sturgeon

sighed heavily. "They never give up, and so they cause a great deal of mischief. They're forever poking their beaks into other people's business."

Misha grinned. The Ancient One sounded just like his grandma.

"I apologize again for bringing you here at night," the sturgeon continued, "but it's the safest time. The crows roost when the light starts to go, and they don't leave their roosts until dawn. Remember that, Misha."

Misha wriggled uncomfortably and wondered what the information had to do with him.

There was a long silence, then the Ancient One spoke again. "Do you know your aunt's full name?"

Misha shut his eyes tightly and tried to remember.

"Dora … Dora … Pandora Betony Elliot," he said triumphantly.

"Have you ever heard the name Pandora before?"

"I'm not sure … kind of a long time ago, I think … in a story?" Misha concentrated. "But I've forgotten what it was about."

The Ancient One nodded sadly. "So much knowledge dismissed," he grumbled. "A story … that's all the humans know … a story."

He swirled around and faced Misha. "There is more to your world than science and technology. More than you could ever dream of knowing. The old stories hide truths. Truths that were never meant to be spoken about. But humans are a strange race — unlike the fish, they can never keep complete counsel. Talk, talk, talk! The cleverest of the Ancients hid the truth in stories for children, so no one suspected. The real truths are kept only for the Chosen Ones of each generation."

Misha was following with difficulty. "Is Dora a Chosen One?"

The Ancient One nodded. "She is the Keeper. She's forbidden to show anyone the secret in her care, but she has helpers she can call upon in times of need."

"You?"

"Yes, and now you!"

Misha felt a knot of panic in his stomach. "What can I do? I'm just a kid."

"Who else can I ask?" the sturgeon grunted. "An adult?"

Misha smiled to himself. Would an adult believe in a talking fish? Would an adult have jumped into the water?

"What makes you think I won't tell?" he asked curiously.

"Tell what?" the Ancient One chuckled rustily. "That you turned into a fish?"

"Right," agreed Misha. "Who'd believe me?"

"No more talking, Misha. We don't have much time ... just listen. In the far distant past there was an Ancient named Pandora. Her task was to look after a large jar, but she didn't know what was inside. Eventually curiosity got the better of her. Pandora uncorked the jar to take a look. Out flew all the evils that now plague the human race. Horrified, Pandora swiftly recorked the jar, but it was too late. The only thing left inside was Hope, who had got stuck under the jar's rim and couldn't get out."

The great white sturgeon spun his ancient tale so vividly that the images flashed through Misha's brain as though on a television screen.

"That's it," interrupted Misha, waggling his fins excitedly. "But it wasn't a jar … it was a box. Pandora's box. I remember the story now!"

"Listen carefully. The humans only remember a children's story. I'll tell you the truth behind it — the part of the story only the fish know! It was a jar. The box came later."

Misha subsided into the gravel bed.

"Now, Pandora had to save humanity, yet she couldn't be seen interfering with the jar. She didn't want the other Ancients to realize what she had done. She swiftly snatched an empty box, transferred

Hope inside and tightly closed the lid. Then she took the box with her everywhere she went. Once each day, without fail, she raised the box lid and let out a tiny bit of Hope to help the humans have strength to fight the evils.

"Eventually, of course, the other Ancients discovered what had happened. But they realized Pandora was trying to right her wrong. They helped her by fitting the box with a special lock to keep Hope safe. So the box could never be opened by accident. Then they made two keys.

"Gradually the race of Ancients faded into the mist of time, but they gave the box and one key to the humans who followed them.

"The box and key were to be passed on to each generation, to the next Keeper. That person's job was to unlock the box each day and deliver some hope to the human world.

"The other key was given to the oldest race of fish, the long-lived sturgeons. Fish are considered quiet, loyal, and trustworthy. They are the keepers of the dark and secret places in the earth. Our ancestors deposited the key in a safe place in the depths of the earth. If the humans ever lost their key, we had a spare. It was placed on the island in this hidden cavern.

"All went well throughout the centuries, until this year.

"Humans dug and blasted in a quarry far above us, until one day the earth shook and caved in. A hole appeared in the ceiling of this cavern. A crow happened to fly overhead at midday when the sun shone directly into the hole. The sunlight glinted on the key lying in the middle of the island. The crow swooped down into the cavern, grabbed the key and flew out again before we realized what had happened."

Misha nodded sagely. "Dora told me crows collect shiny things."

The great fish beside him gave a long bubbling sigh again. "Yes, the crows are acquisitive and curious, and they like power. Their Ancient One — the leader they call Old One — remembered the stories and recognized the key's significance. The crows have been searching for the box at Dora's ever since. They must not find it. If they open the box the wrong way, Hope will disappear forever."

The sturgeon swiveled his nearest eye down toward Misha. "The crows are watching Dora's every move. But a human child who believes the story could get the key back for us. Will you help?"

Chapter Six

"I'll help, if I can," said Misha hesitantly. "But where will I look for the key? It could be … anywhere, right?"

"I think not," said the Ancient One. "We suspect the crows have hidden the key somewhere in the ruins of the mansion near the village. That's where they congregate. If you watch them carefully, you should be able to find out where."

"Okay," agreed Misha, relieved. "I can do that. Dora told me about the ruins, and I'm going to explore them. It shouldn't be too hard to keep an eye on the crows at the same time." He wriggled again uneasily. "Please, can we go back now? It must be nearly morning."

The Ancient One ran a comforting fin across Misha's scales. "I'm sorry. I forget humans find the darkness and depths oppressive. You've done well, Misha. But before you leave, I must warn you, the crows can be mean. They have a leader as old and wily as me. An albino crow they call Old One —"

"A white crow," interrupted Misha. "We found a white feather in the cottage. He must have been inside, searching."

"Then the danger is graver than I thought," said the sturgeon sadly. "He's grown bold. He knows the old stories and is hungry for the power the box might bring. He already has the key. He must not find the box."

Misha waggled agreement.

"You must be prepared for danger, Little One. But be comforted by the fact that crows are forbidden to kill humans."

Misha felt a chill of fear run up his

spine. Any mention of killing sounded bad. Really bad.

"Now, something to help you. First, remember the bell, for it too has forgotten powers."

"But no one knows where it is," protested Misha.

"Oh, you humans!" the sturgeon rumbled in an irritated fashion. "It's quite obvious. Just think of the village name. It tells you all you need to know."

The Ancient One raised a fin as Misha began to speak. "No, don't interrupt, for time is running out. Second, if you need me, call the way Dora did."

"With the 'Alive without breath' riddle?" asked Misha.

"Yes, yes, yes," grumbled the sturgeon. "Only humans would make an ancient spell into a child's riddle." He sighed again. "Yes. Remember the riddle, and I will come."

The great sturgeon curved both ways to look behind him, as though waiting for someone, then turned back to Misha.

"You'll need to watch your tongue and to call upon your personal strengths, Little One. But if all goes well, we should need you only for a short time. Just until we get the key back."

"Does Dora know what's happening to me?" Misha asked.

"Yes. She's swum as a fish too, so she'll understand. Now, one more thing before you leave."

The sturgeon maneuvered his great body until he and Misha were nose to nose. "You must take an oath, an oath of silence, the same oath that Dora took. And you must never, never speak of these matters to any human other than Dora."

"Okay, I'll take the oath, but ... but ... what will happen if I fail?"

The Ancient One fixed Misha with a steely glare. "You mustn't!" He looked around again, then swam in a ghostly circle. "It's time," he said, and headed toward the island. "Follow me."

As they swam slowly across the great

dark lake, Misha became aware of other fish joining them, following slowly and silently behind. By the time they reached the shores of the island, the water pulsed with thousands and thousands of fish jostling for space in a circle around Misha and the Ancient One.

The Ancient One pointed his snout upward. "The moon has left, but first light of dawn will soon appear. We have to hurry. Are you ready, Little One?"

"Guess so. What do I do?" muttered Misha uncertainly.

"Repeat the lines of the oath after me. Then, when I shout, give a great leap upward toward the dawn light. Do you understand?"

Misha nodded.

"The fish would like to thank you for helping us."

One by one, the fish around Misha began splashing the surface of the water with their tails. Gradually every fish joined in, until the water bubbled and foamed.

It tickled Misha's skin and joyously tossed him around topsy-turvy until he was helpless with laughter. Gradually the water subsided and solemnity took over again.

The Ancient One glanced upward again. Misha realized there was the faintest hint of light in the darkness above them. The sturgeon splashed his tail and maneuvered around to face the smaller fish.

Once again the Ancient One and Misha lay nose to nose.

"Now?" the Ancient One asked. Misha nodded.

"I promise," began the Ancient One.

"I promise," Misha repeated each line solemnly.

"To serve and protect in silence.
I promise …
To use the silence of the dark by day.
To use the silence of the dark by night.
And never to divulge
The lore of the Ancients."

There was a long pause as though thousands of fish were holding their breath.

"JUMP," bellowed the sturgeon.

Misha gathered his strength and shot upward. He broke through the surface of the water to meet the first sunbeam from the newly risen sun. It captured him.

With a WHOOSH Misha felt himself sucked through the air in a ball of golden light. He was catapulted over hills and trees and deposited with a slight bump on the flat rock on the edge of Dora's pond.

He stood there shaking and disoriented. He was a boy again. His clothes were dry. He didn't even feel very tired after his long night, just bewildered.

Then a sound made him look around. A distant CAW!

"The crows! They're waking with the dawn." Misha pulled himself together, turned on his heels and, carefully keeping in the shadow of the trees, moved swiftly toward the house. He slipped silently through the kitchen door, crept up the stairs, threw

59

off his clothes and jumped into bed. He lay still with his eyes closed.

Outside, Watcher flew to take up his post in the elder tree.

"CAW, CAW, still asleep, asleep," he called.

Misha smiled to himself, turned over and snuggled into the pillow.

Chapter Seven

It was ten a.m. before Misha woke again. He padded down the servants' stairs and through the cupboard door into the kitchen. He was ready to start the search for the crows' hiding place.

Dora was lifting a fragrant batch of muffins out of the oven. She looked at him sideways. "It's often difficult to sleep in a strange bed. I hope you didn't have too rough a night?"

Misha grinned. So that was the way she was going to play it — as though everything was normal. It was a good way to fool any listening crows.

He shrugged casually. "Not bad. Just crazy dreams. You shouldn't have told me about the elderberry blossoms."

Dora laughed. She expertly flipped a couple of muffins onto a plate and waved Misha to the table.

"So, do you want to explore the village or the park?" she asked.

"Both," said Misha eagerly. "I want to check out the village, then explore ..." He trailed off.

There was a note leaning against his breakfast cup.

We need to talk safely. Be careful around open windows and doors. The crows are everywhere. We'll make an excuse to go to the car or the cellar.

Misha surreptitiously gave Dora a thumbs-up and crumpled the note.

Dora continued the conversation. "Would you like to take a picnic?"

Misha's mouth was full, so he nodded.

"When you've finished breakfast, I'll need

help to get supplies from the cellar." One of Dora's eyelids dropped in a quick wink.

Bubbles of excitement fizzed in Misha's insides, and he gave his leg a pinch. It hurt, so he wasn't dreaming. He was wide awake and the amazing adventure was still continuing.

On the roof above, Watcher listened in dismay to the voices floating up the old stovepipe.

"CAAW, CAAW?" he called worriedly. "The child ... the child. He's going exploring ... exploring. Where's the key ... the key?"

"Safe, safe," came the distant answer.

But Watcher was still uneasy. "CAAW, CAAW, CAAW. Danger, danger, danger," he called.

Swiftwings flew over and they huddled together, whispering and ruffling their feathers.

"I'll tell the others. Be ready ... ready," muttered Swiftwings, and flew off.

Relieved, Watcher cocked his head toward the stovepipe again. He heard scraping and clunking sounds, and the creak of a door.

"Come and show me what I can take for lunch." Misha's voice floated thinly up the stovepipe.

There were a few footsteps, then silence.

With a frustrated "CAW" Watcher flapped over to the elder tree so he could see through the kitchen window. He was just in time to spot Dora's head disappearing below floor level.

"CAW CAW ..." Watcher ruffled up his feathers in dismay.

Dora and Misha perched on the packing cases.

Dora chose her words carefully. "You met my old friend?" Her voice was only a whisper of sound.

Misha tried to copy her. "Yes, and I

promised to help," he hissed back.

"Then we need a plan of action. The crows know about me, but they aren't sure about you. Because they're uneasy, they will be watching you carefully."

Misha nodded thoughtfully. "But if I'm a regular kid on holiday, I would be exploring and climbing trees and fishing and stuff."

"Exactly ... and that's how you'll behave. But keep your eyes open all the time."

Dora dropped her voice even further and leaned toward Misha's ear. "My key is safe." She fiddled under the neckline of her dress. "It never leaves me." She pulled out a long gold chain. Hanging on the end was a tiny, beautifully carved gold key.

Misha reverently held out his palm.

Dora laid the key on it. "The key you are looking for is sister to this."

"It's beautiful," breathed Misha. "I won't mistake it for a regular key."

Dora dropped the key back inside her dress. "The box is well protected too."

"Where?" asked Misha. "Which one is it?"

Dora grinned wickedly. "If you don't know, you will never be able to tell."

"Oh!" Misha's face fell, then brightened. "So that's why you collect boxes? So people will never guess that one is extra special? Wow." He looked admiringly at his aunt, then almost fell off the packing case. His whisper grew louder in his excitement. "Hey, I've an idea. Let's use one as a decoy."

"Shhhhh," reminded Dora, then echoed his words. "A decoy?"

"Yup. Hide a box, any old box, in here, like I did. You could do it kind of sneakily. But make sure a crow can see you. Let them think it's THE box. To put them off the scent."

Dora looked at Misha with delight and gave him a hug. "Great idea. I knew you'd be an asset." She thought for a moment. "I'll be a decoy too. I'll hide a box, then *I'll* go exploring. Let them think *I'm* the one searching for the key. The crows should follow me and not you."

"Awesome," approved Misha.

Dora stood up, swiftly gathered some things off the shelves and thrust a couple of jars in Misha's hands. "Carry these. If we stay down here too long, the crows will be suspicious of you."

"Oh, Aunt Dora," hissed Misha as an afterthought. "Ancient One said the bell would help. We should look for that too."

Dora nodded and started up the steps, talking loudly over her shoulder. "The village is fun but small. It won't take you long to walk through. In fact, maybe I'll come with you."

Misha caught on and clambered noisily up the steps behind her. "Great. I'd like that."

"I'll show you the park," continued Dora, "and you can explore it on your own. You'll enjoy the park. It was once a millionaire's estate. And the house that used to stand in the grounds was called 'Luck-ee-Nuff.'"

Misha chuckled. "Bad pun."

"The millionaire was a true eccentric," said Dora, placing her haul of cans on the kitchen counter. "He loved secret passages and tunnels, and he built them all along the riverbank and into the hill the house stood on."

"Can I go in the tunnels?" asked Misha as he watched Dora begin to make the sandwiches.

Dora shook her head. "No. The park officials boarded up the entrances and placed bars across the window openings." She paused as a loud cawing from the tree outside the window distracted her.

Dora turned her back to the window and dropped her voice as she walked over to Misha to take a jar of peanut butter from his arms. "It is said there was still a way in if you knew where to look," she whispered. "But it's probably just that — a rumor."

Blackwings, a young crow, circled down

to the elder tree and joined Watcher.

"CAW ... CAW ... Secret Room ... watch ... watch ..." Watcher reported.

Two sets of beady eyes stared unblinking as Dora and Misha closed the cellar door and replaced the rug and the table.

"They're going exploring, exploring," Watcher called. "We must scare them ... scare them."

"Scare them ... scare them," agreed Blackwings.

Both crows fell silent. Watching.

Misha prepared for the day's adventure by carefully stocking his backpack. He prowled around the kitchen, collecting the lunch Dora had made, a drink, an extra snack, a sweater in case he became chilled, and a flashlight to shine through the window bars and see into the Luck-ee-Nuff tunnels. Finally, he tucked in a sketched map of the village and park.

Dora sat, as though deep in thought, at the kitchen table. She absently sipped a cup of coffee and occasionally drummed her fingers on its edge.

Finally Dora stood up. "There is something I must do," she announced abruptly. "I'll need help moving the table again before we leave." She went upstairs.

Misha felt the flicker of excitement burn inside him. Their plan had begun. From the corner of his eye, he saw the leaves of the elder tree stir as a crow fluttered to a higher branch that overlooked an upstairs window.

Dora reappeared in the kitchen carrying a small box-like shape half concealed in the folds of her skirt. She moved over to the kitchen counter. Shielding it from Misha with her body, she fiddled in a drawer and brought out a brown paper bag. Misha caught a glimpse of a shiny tin set with sparkling colored glass jewels before Dora slipped it inside the bag and folded the top over.

"What's that?" asked Misha, playing along.

"Oh, just something I felt might be best in a safe place while we're out," Dora answered. "Could you lift that end of the table again?"

★★★

In the elder tree, Blackwings was so excited he nearly lost his perch.

"CAW, CAW, CAW … See it … see it … see it? THE BOX, THE BOX!"

"Shiny, shiny," approved Watcher.

"Must tell Old One … tell Old One …" stuttered Blackwings.

Watcher shook his head. "Patience … Watch longer … longer … longer."

Both crows glared in the kitchen window as Dora disappeared into the cellar carrying the bag, and reappeared empty-handed.

"Can't get it now. Impossible … impossible." Watcher clacked his beak angrily as Dora and Misha replaced the rug and

table once again.

"They're coming out ... out," observed Blackwings.

The crows watched Misha put on his pack, then he and Dora disappeared, only to reappear in the garden a moment later, shutting the back door.

"Scare them ... scare them," Watcher ordered.

"Scare them ... scare them ... SCARE THEM." Blackwings screamed and dived out of the elder, flapping and cawing right in Misha's and Dora's faces. Dora staggered back, but Misha stumbled down the back steps. Dora shot out her hand and saved him before he fell flat on his face.

"CAW," approved Watcher, as Blackwings headed across the field, screaming for reinforcements.

Chapter Eight

"That crow was really scary." Misha rubbed his knees where they had hit the step.

Dora gave his shoulders a comforting squeeze. "It was just trying to frighten us."

"It worked!" Misha readjusted his pack. They walked down the garden path together, toward the gate. "I hate them."

Misha was glad Dora was with him. He dreaded looking for the key on his own. Suddenly the longed-for adventure wasn't fun.

They walked around the small village trying to make normal conversation while surreptitiously looking for the bell. They checked the church, the inn, and an antique store. Dora pointed out interesting things along the way, to distract listening crows, and Misha tried to laugh and joke as though nothing was wrong. Several people waved to Dora, but to Misha's relief she didn't stop to chat.

They bought ice cream cones from the village store, walked to a bus-stop bench on the outskirts of the village and sat down.

They were quite alone, and there were no concealing trees nearby. Only one crow cruised above, high in the sky.

Dora squinted up at it. "I suspect that one is keeping an eye on us."

Misha only grunted in agreement. He was feeling depressed. Gone was the exhilaration of the nighttime swim with the old sturgeon. In its place was a dislike of the crows, and a deep fear that he was not going to be able to outwit them. He tried to gather his thoughts together. "Your house is the only place in the village where the crows gather."

Dora nodded her agreement.

"And they haven't bothered us so far."

Dora nodded again. "Obviously, there is nothing around here to worry them."

Misha stood, a determined look on his face. "Then I guess we'd better go to the park and get it over with. See what area they are protecting."

"We can't talk when the crows are around. Let's make a plan now," Dora suggested. "Where's the map?"

Misha dropped his pack on the seat, unzipped a pocket and pulled out the map.

Dora's finger pointed out the trails and several features in the park. "I'll come with you until we get to the lake, then we'll split up. It will be natural for you to go to the side with the ruins — that's where all visitors go. I'll sneak around the other lakeshore as if searching for something. Hopefully the crows will be so busy following me, they'll leave you alone."

"Hope so." Misha wasn't convinced.

But he straightened his shoulders. "Okay. Let's go."

Outwardly, Misha and Dora walked calmly down the hill to the park, but inwardly, Misha was seething. It was hard to behave normally. With every rustle in the trees, he was aware of the crows, watching and listening.

The stream bubbled and chortled beside them, then tumbled in a series of steep waterfalls down the valley sides and into the river. Misha hung over a wall to watch the water swirl and eddy below. He vividly remembered its feel on his scales and the scent of the information it carried as it rushed through his gills.

Three crows flapped slowly overhead.

Misha and Dora tensed.

Suddenly the crows gave raucous cries and swooped down to the road.

Horrified, Misha realized the crows had spotted a dead raccoon that had been hit by a car. He retreated several paces.

Two crows landed on the raccoon and

started pecking at it. The third stood in the road cawing wildly, glaring at Misha and Dora.

In response to the calls, crow after crow glided in and landed on, or by, the raccoon's body. Soon the center of the road was black with over a hundred crows, pushing, squawking and tearing at the carcass. The crows that were unable to reach the body turned and glared, croaked and hopped threateningly toward Misha and Dora.

Misha and Dora edged further away. More crows approached them, flapping their wings and clattering their wicked black beaks.

Suddenly Dora drew herself up tall and straight. She raised her arms in the air in a great V. It was as if a cloak of light fell over her and Misha.

"No closer!" she shouted.

The crows froze and fell silent.

A car swept down the road. The crows flew up and dispersed with the cloud of exhaust fumes.

Sickened and trembling, and aware that war had been declared, Misha and Dora ran hand in hand from the road and entered the park.

Swiftwings flapped along slowly, high overhead. Dora was a known entity, but the human child made him nervous. He wanted to keep a careful eye on the child's movements.

"They're in the park ... the park," he warned.

Several CAWS echoed through the valley as other crows answered.

"We see ... we see."

Despite Dora's comforting presence, Misha shivered as they passed through the park gate and took the path by the river. He felt a prickling sensation at the back of his neck, an awareness of the hundreds of hidden eyes watching him. He looked at the trees lining the bank, but the leaves were too thick to see much. There was just a hint of glossy black bodies perched in the shadows. The birds were still and silent.

The sullen silence continued as Misha and Dora penetrated deeper into the park. Misha noticed the remains of stone walkways and castle-like walls protruding from the opposite riverbank. He paused and looked with astonishment across at a turret with a round window and its own small balcony.

"If the riverbank is riddled with spots like that, there must be a million hiding places for a small key," said Misha, discouraged. "How can I possibly check them all?"

The trees thinned and the grassy banks ran down to the water's edge. Here the river was suddenly diverted. It widened, deepened and swirled against dam gates, then rushed sideways through a mysterious underground tunnel in the far bank. Beyond, spread a large, shallow, ornamental lake. A bridge ran over the dam. Two crows sat on posts at the far side.

Misha nudged Dora with his elbow. She gave a tiny nod.

Dora pointed past the bridge and the sentinel crows. "That's where the ruins are, if you would like to see them," she said, her voice a little strained. "I have something I'd like to check out on this side of the lake. I'll meet you back here in about an hour, okay?"

"Okay." Misha made himself smile and give a carefree wave. "I should get an Oscar for this," he thought as he forced himself to step casually onto the bridge toward the crows.

The two crows spread their wings, left their posts and flew over his head toward Dora.

Misha turned and watched. Dora was moving rapidly down the lakeside path. She gave a last wave and disappeared into the trees on the far side. The two crows set up an urgent cawing, and another dozen crows rose from the branches of a nearby tree and joined them. They all followed Dora.

A flood of relief washed over Misha. The plan was working.

Misha paused to look at the dam gates below him. They were old and warped, gigantic wooden gates held firmly in place by ornate iron bars. Misha could see no handles or pins to open them, but they easily held back the water.

Misha jumped down the steps from the bridge. He found himself among the remains of a garden. Crumbling stone walls held back overgrown banks, and flights of uneven stone stairs disappeared up into the forest, their adjoining paths fading into dense undergrowth. A wide expanse of daisy-covered grass ran from the bridge to the lake edge. A great green fountain rose from the middle of the lawn.

Intrigued, Misha ran over to it and stood gazing up.

Three concrete basins rose in tiers to twice his height. Each brimmed with stagnant water, which oozed slowly over the side to fall in the basin below. The outside of each basin was coated with a thick layer of brilliant green moss. There was some kind of ornament on the fountain top, but it was so concealed with green moss that its shape was unrecognizable.

"This must be the fountain Dora told me about," Misha muttered to himself. "It's big and fancy … it must be what gave the village its name. Belle fountain — beautiful fountain — but I wonder why no one has ever cleaned the moss off."

As Misha looked thoughtfully at the fountain, something jogged his memory.

As clear as anything, he heard the Ancient One's voice. *Remember the Bell, for it too has forgotten powers … It's quite obvious. Just think of the village name. It tells you all you need to know.*

"Wow," Misha gasped. "It *is* obvious. Not belle fountain, but BELL fountain." He quickly glanced around. The park seemed completely empty. No people. No crows.

Swiftly Misha leaped onto the edge of the fountain's first basin and grasped the edge of the second.

The moss was slippery. He teetered for a moment, but he managed to retain his balance. He stretched over the slime-covered water to get his knee onto the edge of the second basin. With a quick movement he pulled himself precariously up on its edge. Carefully he stood upright and slowly reached past the smallest basin to the ornamental top.

"CAW, CAW ... CAW, CAW ... the fountain, fountain ..."
Swiftwings broke from the trees on the opposite side of the lake and flew in a great circle of panic.

Misha glanced up briefly but turned

his attention back to the fountain top. Balancing carefully, he grasped a chunk of moss and pulled. It came away easily. The sunlight glinted on a hint of brass beneath. He tossed the moss onto the ground and pulled again. Then he used both hands to peel off great chunks.

"CAW, CAW, CAW, CAW ... alarm ... ALARM!"

Other crows appeared and joined in Swiftwings's frantic dash across the lake.

Misha redoubled his effort and gave a pleased grunt as the last piece of moss came away in his hands.

The green fountain was now topped by a beautiful brass bell that gleamed in the sunlight.

"Yes!" cried Misha triumphantly.

The bell's smooth surface reflected a movement. Misha looked up uneasily to see dozens of crows speeding toward him.

He started to climb down, slipped and grabbed the bell.

It swung away from him with a great DONG.

Misha lost his balance and half slithered, half tumbled down from the fountain.

DONG, DONG.

Thousands of crows rose like smoke from every tree in the park.

Dazedly, Misha checked himself to see if he was all right. He rubbed his ankles, patted his chest — nothing sprained or broken. Then he wiped the moss and slime off his face and shirt. He was okay.

DONG, DONG, the bell continued to peal.

Misha stared up in terror.

The sky was black with crows, all looking down at him and cawing wildly. As he watched, horrified, they massed together and began to stream toward him in a great black arrow.

Misha turned to run across the grass to the bridge.

DONG, DONG, DONG, DONG.

As the bell pealed insistently, a grinding

of ancient machinery rumbled below the ground. An answering creak and grind came from beneath the bridge. Misha watched with disbelief as the old dam gates slowly opened. The tunnel gates closed, and with a roar the entire river spewed into the lake. The lake rapidly began to rise. It overflowed the low banks, lapped around the steps of the bridge and crept across the grass.

When the bell rings, the river is supposed to rise and encircle the village to keep it safe. This time it was Dora's voice Misha recalled. But it was no comfort. The flood wasn't helping; it was between him and the bridge. So were the crows.

The crows were almost upon him, their dagger-like beaks pointed dangerously in Misha's direction. He paused, disoriented by the raucous cries, the roar of the water, and the clanging of the bell.

Misha swiveled and changed direction. Head down and with his backpack over his head and neck for protection, he ran toward the uneven steps he'd passed earlier. He had no idea why the flood was making the crows so angry, but he needed to get away from them fast!

SLAM ... SLAM. Time and time again, the crows angrily dive-bombed Misha, smashing into his shoulders and back with their bodies and whizzing around his ankles to trip him.

Misha could hear the whoosh of their wings as the crows swarmed around him. Each second he expected to feel a razor-sharp beak stabbing him. He was grateful for the protection of the pack.

DONG, DONG, DONG. The incessant ringing of the bell pounded terrifyingly through Misha's brain. Stumbling, and gasping with fright, he leaped desperately up the crumbling stone staircase, two steps at a time. He scrambled over a bank and dived headfirst into the undergrowth. Burrowing frantically, he forced his way uphill, following the remains of an overgrown path.

The cries faded as the crows banked away and wheeled upward, foiled by the dense shrubbery hiding Misha.

Misha lay very still in the middle of the green and brown tunnel of undergrowth. Bushes and briars arched comfortingly over his body, hiding and cocooning him. His heart was pounding so badly it was almost jumping out of his chest. He tried to stop gasping noisily for air, but his lungs were bursting. He was splayed against the loamy earth, twigs pricking his scalp, the taste of dirt in his mouth and nostrils, and his hands and fingers scratched and bleeding. Chest heaving, Misha closed his eyes and lay for a long time.

Silence finally roused him.

Misha lifted his head and listened. No crows, no bell, no rushing water. Just the occasional stirring of leaves far above and the buzz of insects around his ears.

He looked ahead, along the remains of the old path. It was a well-defined, low tunnel through the undergrowth, obviously used by small animals. It seemed to continue uphill.

If I can get to the top I might be able to see what's happening without being spotted, he thought.

Misha gave an exploratory wriggle and edged forward, but the tunnel had narrowed. His backpack was catching. He eased it off, one shoulder at a time, and pushed it ahead of him. Now, by wriggling on his belly, he could just fit through the tunnel without disturbing the low-growing branches.

Slowly Misha crept upward, until he reached a curved wall of stones cemented together and covered with ivy. The trees and shrubs thinned slightly at its edge, leaving him room to stand up. Misha slowly rose and cautiously peered between the tree branches.

He was on a ridge of land overlooking the valley. The lake spread below. It was gigantic now, completely covering the lawn and surrounding the fountain. Hundreds of crows were flying around in disarray, swooping down to check the dam and rising up again to circle in the sky. None of them were looking his way.

Misha edged around the curve of the wall but stumbled over a tree root. He thrust out his hand to grasp the ivy and steady himself, but the ivy swung inward. He tumbled headlong through a gap.

With a soft swish, the ivy swung back and concealed him.

Chapter Nine

"Where am I?" It was too gloomy for Misha to make sense of his surroundings. He sat up stretched his arm toward the ivy and pulled some aside.

Small patches of light dappled the floor of a curved stone room.

"I must be in one of the Luck-ee-Nuff caves." Misha crawled cautiously over to the ivy curtain, parted it further and carefully peered through. His pack lay some paces away. He leaned out, grabbed it and swiftly dragged it inside the cave. He fumbled in one of its pockets for his flashlight.

The beam comfortingly illuminated stone walls with benches built into the sides and a recessed archway in the back. There was no wall on one side, just the thick ivy curtain.

"Fantastic — this must have been some kind of summerhouse that's become totally overgrown and forgotten." Misha placed his pack on the bench and walked around.

The beam from the flashlight swept over a roof laced with spiderwebs and the remains of old swallow nests. Dead leaves and twigs made a crunchy floor covering, but there were no signs of recent human usage and no hint that the crows had ever been inside. Misha gave a sigh of relief. He sat on one of the benches to reassess the situation.

"Dora said there was a rumor of a tunnel entrance that the park officials missed. Maybe this is it." Misha turned his flashlight to the archway at the back of the cave. The beam illuminated a sturdy-looking wooden door with a heavy metal latch.

There was no visible lock.

Misha walked over and hesitantly pressed the latch. Nothing happened. He gently kicked the base of the door. The thud echoed dully, and a large black beetle scurried out of a crack at the bottom and raced across the floor to hide under the bench.

"Sorry," muttered Misha, and he jiggled the latch again. It seemed to move a fraction, so he leaned all his weight on it and felt it give. The metal bar rose out of its socket, and Misha pushed hard against the wood. The door remained closed.

Misha stood back and ran his flashlight beam around the edge of the door. It was flat to the wall. "Of course," he muttered. "If people were coming from a tunnel, they'd enter from the other side." He raised the latch again and, instead of pushing, pulled hard. Slowly, and with only the faintest of creaks, the door opened. Beyond it, a passageway sloped downward toward steps that curved into darkness.

Misha walked back to the curtain of

ivy and peeked out again.

A solitary crow flapped overhead.

Misha retreated fast, sat on the bench and looked at the open door.

"At some point, I'll have to get back home," he mused. "But if I go back now, I may never find the key for the sturgeon."

The passageway looked very black.

"I can't get back the way I came. So I'm going have to find another way."

The passageway looked a little more acceptable.

"And I'd rather go down an unknown passage than face those crazy crows."

By this time, the dark passage looked positively inviting.

Misha shouldered his pack, firmly grasped his flashlight and passed through the doorway.

Inside wasn't as scary as he'd anticipated. The steps were well made, and there was a metal handrail fixed to the wall. A faint draft of air stirred the hair on his forehead, so Misha knew there was some sort of opening at the other end. Step by careful step, he descended. The steps spiraled downward, then leveled out again. By this time Misha had lost all sense of direction. His world was confined to the few yards illuminated by the flashlight.

Suddenly he heard a caw ahead of him. Misha froze and instinctively switched off the light. He flinched as the darkness pressed all around him.

"CAW, CAW ... treasure still safe, still safe," the albino crow croaked reassuringly to a younger crow who had come to check on him. "Where's the boy, the boy?"

The young crow shrugged, and Old One clacked his beak in displeasure.

"Flood stopped ... stopped," the young crow offered.

Old One sighed with relief.

"Then I'll come, come."

"Look for the boy ... SEARCH, SEARCH ... search, search ..."

Cawing loudly, the two crows flew off, leaving a heavy silence behind.

In the darkness, Misha stirred stiffly. He'd not dared to move while he could hear the crows, but now they'd flown away. He risked switching on the flashlight, though he shielded it with his shirt so it illuminated only a small area at his feet. He stepped forward one pace at a time, hand on the wall to steady himself. The wall curved, and as Misha edged around, a faint glimmer of daylight appeared.

Misha paused, switched off the flashlight and listened intently.

He could hear the gentle lapping of water close by, and a very faint rustling of trees. Nothing else.

Carefully he edged around the corner and found himself behind a half-open door. He peeked through the gap by the hinges.

He was looking down into a flooded room several steps below him. Both water and daylight entered through a barred entrance overlooking the lake. The flood water filled the room, lapping up to the top edge of a stone table in the center.

"No wonder the crows were so upset when the flood started," breathed Misha. "They were scared their treasure hoard would be washed away."

The top of the stone table was covered with the crows' treasure. Metal bottle caps, aluminum tabs from beer and pop cans, brightly colored candy wrappers, pieces of aluminum foil, glass beads, rings, and necklaces were all heaped together in a gleaming pile. Small waves washed against the tabletop, and floating twigs, leaves, and other debris caught and pulled at the items along the edge.

Misha crept out from behind the door, stood on the top step and surveyed the room. He dumped his pack and laid the flashlight on top. He took off his run-

ners, tied them together and slung them around his neck. Hitching his jeans up as far as they would go, he stepped cautiously into the water with one foot. The water was only knee high. He could wade out to the table.

Confidently he stepped forward, missed his footing on a broken step and fell under with a loud SPLASH.

Coughing and spluttering with shock, Misha kicked out and found another step. He regained his footing and stood up. Water streamed down his body.

He dragged a hand over his eyes and face, coughed and spat.

"Uuurgh! Disgusting."

He looked at the dirty, swirling water. He didn't mind swimming, but this water was the pits. Gritting his teeth, he felt his way carefully down the hidden stairs. The water was chest high. Misha half waded, half swam across the room until he reached the table.

Rapidly he surveyed the crows' treasure.

It was a tremendous hodgepodge of rubbish, with a small aluminum pie plate upended exactly in the middle. Misha lifted the plate. Underneath was a tiny, beautifully carved gold key.

"YES!" he crowed in triumph.

As he stretched out his hand, a young crow fluttered in through the bars.

With a squawk of terror, it dived toward Misha and jabbed at his hand, drawing blood across the knuckle.

Misha yelled and dropped the key back into the pile of litter on the table. He flailed around with his other arm to ward off the crow while he tried to pick it up again. Once more the key slipped from his grasp.

Wings beat around Misha's head. Water splashed in his eyes. Slipping, cursing, yelling, and trying to beat off the crow, Misha leaned over the table, shielding the treasure with his body, and concentrated on finding the key.

There it was, intertwined with some chains and keys. Misha grabbed the whole handful and rammed it in his jeans pocket. Treasure fell in chunks off the table. The young crow cawed in distress.

Swiftly Misha swam back to the steps. Time and time again, the young crow dive-bombed his head, and Misha had to duck under the filthy water. Half blinded, with the water streaming down his face, Misha staggered up the stairs and grabbed the only weapon at hand — his flashlight.

He flung it desperately at the oncoming crow.

The flashlight hit one side of the crow's head with a soft THUNK, then dropped into the water and disappeared from view. A few feathers floated down and landed on the surface.

The crow stumbled in mid-flight and fell clumsily to the table. It landed hard on top of the treasure, dislodging a few more pieces. It lay there, dazed.

Misha grabbed his pack and rushed through the doorway. He placed his back against the open door, braced his feet against the floor and began to push. Slowly the door began to move. It shut with a bang. The darkness was instantaneous.

Dust and cobwebs rained down from the roof like black snow. Misha shook his head to dislodge them. Then reaction set in. He sank to the ground with a sob. What had he done? He was soaking wet, cut and bruised, and in total darkness. He'd no flashlight and no shoes — they'd disappeared during one of the dunkings.

Wave upon wave of fear made Misha tremble. The terrifying darkness pressed down on him. The walls seemed to move in, and his bones turned to jelly. Somehow, he had to find his way up the pitch-black passage and back into the upper room.

The task seemed impossible.

It's all right, Little One. The echo of the giant sturgeon's voice rumbled through his despair. *Don't be frightened, just think like a fish, and follow me.*

Misha's shoulders straightened as he remembered his night underwater with the fish. It had been black then, pitch black, but his fish senses had made it bearable. If only he could use them now.

Slowly he lifted his head and stared at the darkness before him. *Think like a fish ... think like a fish ... think like a fish ...*

Stiffly Misha stumbled to his feet. In his mind's eye he tried to visualize the passage. He clutched his pack firmly in his left hand. He held out his right hand, palm forward, and concentrated on his fish senses.

Think like a fish ... think like a fish ... think like a fish ...

Step by careful step, Misha inched forward. He discovered his hand could sense a wall before touching it. The drafts of air on his palm also indicated the way the passage twisted and turned.

Think like a fish ... think like a fish ... think like a fish ...

The darkness became bearable, full of smells and feelings that gave Misha's brain information. Slowly, like a child learning to walk, Misha wound his way up the staircase.

His heart rejoiced when his new-found senses told him the surface was only a step or two away.

A glimmer of gray! Misha burst triumphantly through the doorway and into the dimness of the upper cave. After the blackness, it seemed as bright as midday.

Despite his exertions, Misha was shivering. He stripped off his wet jeans and shirt, wrung them out and spread them to dry across the stone benches. He opened his backpack and pulled on his sweater. Suddenly ravenous, he sat on the bench and devoured his sandwiches.

Unearthly shrieks shattered the silence. Thousands of crows were calling in desperation.

"CAW, CAW, CAAAAW ... GONE, GONE, GOOOOONE ..."

Misha covered his ears to lessen the din.

"Uh-oh. The little crow has recovered and told them the key's gone. Now how do I escape?"

Misha dropped his sandwich on top

of his pack and padded over to his jeans. He tipped the handful of treasure out onto the bench and picked up the key. "For something so small, you've sure caused a heap of trouble." He tucked it carefully back in his jeans pocket and returned to his sandwich.

The crows roost when the light starts to go, and they don't leave their roosts until dawn. Remember that, Misha. Once again the Ancient One's voice echoed in Misha's head.

Misha sighed. Obviously, he was stuck here until after sunset. He hoped Dora wouldn't worry. He padded across to the ivy curtain and gently broke off some strands so that enough afternoon sunlight filtered into the cave to comfort him. Then he curled up on the bench, his head on the backpack, to wait until dusk.

Chapter Ten

Once more Misha slithered on his belly back through the overgrown paths and down toward the lake.

The twilight shadows altered everything. It all looked unfamiliar. But what might have been a terrifying journey seemed easy after his experience in the black passage. Misha was just anxious to be home. He worried about Dora. She wouldn't know if he was safe.

An owl hooted. Misha heard a flurry of scuffling sounds in the bushes around him. He tensed, aware now of the number of unseen animals prowling the park at night. He wondered if they were friendly.

Misha's hand hurt, his arms ached, and his face was scratched and bleeding from thorns and twigs. The bruises on his knees protested every push forward. Eventually he reached the top of the crumbling steps. He huddled in the concealing shadows to survey the scene.

No crows were around. The dam gates were closed. The flood water had receded and the lake was back to normal. Only large, dark puddles in the grass remained from the flood. He should have no trouble running across the lawn to the bridge and the way back home.

Misha eased out of the bushes, sat on the steps to reshoulder his pack, then stepped out of the shadows and hurried across the lawn.

From his roost at the top of the fountain, the albino crow watched, his eyes red and full of anger.

"CAW," came the command.

The hair rose on Misha's neck. He turned, like a robot, to look up at the fountain.

The Old One spread his ghostly white wings. The moon slid out from a cloud and intensified his whiteness. His black shadow raced across the grass to enfold Misha.

Misha trembled. "No more. Please, no more."

There was a power here he could not deal with. "Help," he screamed silently in his head. "Someone help me." And suddenly Dora's spell filled his mind.

Misha took a deep breath and yelled in defiance,

"Alive without breath
As cold as death
Never thirsty, always drinking
Clad in mail but never clinking
Ancient One, hear my cry
Help me so that Hope won't die."

There was an answering flash of white from the center of the lake. The ancient sturgeon leaped from the surface of the

water, then re-entered with a loud splash.

With a great CAAW of rage, the albino crow took to the air.

Adrenalin flooded Misha's body. He ran to the edge of the lake and thrust his hand in his pocket to find the golden key.

He pulled it out and held it up in the moonlight.

"I got it, Ancient One … catch!"

Misha threw the key as hard and as far as he could toward the center of the water.

With a CAW of despair, the albino crow folded his wings and dove like a white arrow to intercept the airborne key.

The great white sturgeon circled just below the surface. Then he shot upward in a gigantic leap. With a SNAP of his jaws, he caught the key, just before the crow reached it.

Misha gasped with horror as the beak of the albino crow sliced deeply into the back of the sturgeon. One of the sturgeon's spines pierced the breast of the crow. Old One and Ancient One locked together. Thrashing wildly, the two disappeared below the surface of the lake.

"Misha, Misha," came a soft cry. Misha turned around to see Dora running swiftly over the bridge. She enfolded him in her arms until he stopped shuddering.

★★★

Misha didn't remember stumbling home, supported by Dora. But he woke early the next morning, safely cocooned in his warm bed, surrounded by the smell of cooking bacon and fresh bread.

He stretched and walked stiffly downstairs.

"Good," said Dora, pointing to the backyard. "I was hoping you would wake up soon. An old friend is patiently waiting to see you."

Misha rushed outside to the pond. There lay the Ancient One, a gaping wound on his back.

"I thought you were dead," gulped Misha as he threw himself down on the overhanging rock. He reached out to gently stroke the ancient sturgeon's nose. "You really *are* hurt this time."

The ancient fish grunted and blew a stream of bubbles. "Yes, last evening was definitely my final fight."

"The key … it's safe?" asked Misha.

The old fish gave a toothy grin. "It will always be safe. My time is close. My bones will guard it in the lowest depths of the Deep. Only the trusty fish will ever be able to find it, should it be needed. That is how it was meant to be. The old order is restored again."

"And the crows?" asked Misha.

"The crows have learned their lesson," replied the Ancient One. He rubbed his side against the overhanging rock. Several scales peeled off and floated to the surface. "Choose three of my fish scales, Misha."

Misha reached out and plucked them from the surface of the water. They lay like large pearly sequins in the palm of his hand.

"You and I must part now, Misha. With

my going, I will give you three gifts, symbolized by these scales. The first is the gift of forgetfulness."

"But I don't want to forget," cried Misha.

"The lore of the Ancients is not for everyone," replied the sturgeon. "You may have a different role ahead. It will be difficult for you to grow up normally if these memories haunt your childhood. But if all goes as Dora and I expect, memory will return when you reach adulthood. Do you trust me?"

Misha nodded slowly.

"The second is the gift of understanding. Though you won't remember swimming with me, you will always retain special understanding of the world of the fish. You will be able to use this knowledge to great advantage ... maybe studying to become an important biologist."

Misha chuckled. "You're kidding!"

"The third gift is the most important ... you will always have Hope."

"I ... I don't understand," said Misha.

"No, but one day you will. Dora will know when … Goodbye Misha, my friend, and thank you."

"Goodbye, goodbye," stammered Misha with tears in his eyes. An ache he didn't fully understand filled his heart.

The Ancient One swirled uneasily around the pond as though waiting for something.

Silently Dora joined them.

She knelt down at the water's edge and stretched forth her hands in blessing.

The giant fish lay still. "My time has come — I must pass on," he rumbled.

"I know, my friend," whispered Dora. "May the peace of the dark be always with you."

The great white sturgeon gave a last leap high into the air. His body shimmered and gleamed in the morning light — and for a single instant, Misha and Dora saw him as he'd been in his prime. Smooth and white, sleek and bright, his body glowed as it curved in the air, then dove into the Deep with a silvery splash.

Misha's sadness welled up and burst forth in a howl of despair. Drops of water showered over him like refreshing rain. With the shower came forgetfulness, but still a sense of something unfinished.

Misha held his hand out. "Dora, I found these beautiful fish scales floating on the surface of the pond. Can I add them to the box in our secret room?"

Together they returned to the kitchen, moved the table and lifted the door. Misha retrieved the enameled soldier box, added the fish scales and stowed it safely away again for future use. Feeling oddly satisfied, he returned to the kitchen, where he and Dora replaced the table and ate breakfast together.

The house was full of a sense of peace and well-being.

It was just before dawn. The world was still sleeping when Dora glided to the rock above the pond and stood waiting, as she always waited, for the first glint of light from the sun.

She held a small, battered wooden box in one hand and a tiny golden key in the other. As the dawn broke, she swiftly inserted the key in the lock and turned it, lifted the lid a crack and offered the box toward the rosy light.

A smell of orange blossom filled the air and a chorus of birds began to sing.

Dora closed the lid and locked it, dropping the key on its chain down the neck of her dress.

She silently re-entered the house and replaced the box where it had always lived, by the sink. It looked like an ordinary, well-used, but very old recipe box.

And there it stayed until Misha came of age.

But that's another story.

Author Note

This story sprouted during an idyllic week staying in The Gingerbread Cottage in the historic village of Belfountain, Ontario.

Yes, the cottage is real; so is the door in the floor and the pond in the back garden. The village of Belfountain really does have a stream running beside the road, tumbling down to the beautiful Credit River. But although it is full of trout, I've never seen a great white sturgeon there.

A parklike nature reserve is in the Credit River valley. It contains the remains of the summer home of an eccentric millionaire who built stone grottoes, stairways and secret chambers into the riverbanks. I walked through the park, past the bell-topped fountain, and peered between the bars of an underground grotto. "What a wonderful place to set a children's story," I whispered to myself.

Of course, readers who live in Belfountain know the place well. They will know that my imagination took over and changed the topography, the ruins, the river, and the dam. That's what fiction is all about

— starting from a good idea, then stretching, expanding, and exaggerating it to make a story work.

A novel needs several threads. Readers may recognize the story of Pandora's box, although I am not sure how many will know that, in the original Greek, it was a jar — not a box — that Pandora broke. It is my favorite Greek myth. One day while looking at a particularly beautiful box I own, I wondered what happened to Pandora's box. What if it had survived throughout out the centuries? What would its role be in our modern world?

The great white sturgeon in the story belongs to an ancient group of fish, and individuals live a long time. The sturgeon in my story needed a special "spell" to call it. The first four lines of Dora's spell is one of the oldest riddles in the English language. The answer to the riddle is … a fish.

Every good story needs a villain. Once, while I was on a picnic, a crow (who had been eyeing me for some time) took advantage of my inattention and pinched my sandwiches. It wasn't an accident. He planned it! I was so intrigued by this evidence of intellect that I did some research and found out that crows are indeed intelligent. They not only steal food, but also shiny objects. They are cheeky and fearless, and will mob and divebomb humans who threaten them.

Suddenly all the ideas were in place, and, over the course of a year, *The Keeper and the Crows* almost wrote itself.

Andrea Spalding